S0-DPG-192

JONAH AND THE WHALE

Retold by Mary Packard
Illustrated by Nancy Pistone

A GOLDEN BOOK • NEW YORK
Western Publishing Company, Inc., Racine, Wisconsin 53404

© 1996 Western Publishing Company, Inc. Illustrations © 1996 Nancy Pistone. All rights reserved. Printed in the U.S.A. No part of this book may be reproduced or copied in any form without written permission from the publisher. All trademarks are the property of Western Publishing Company, Inc. Library of Congress Catalog Card Number: 95-78033 ISBN: 0-307-10013-8   MCMXCVI

Long ago, in the land of Israel, God spoke to a man named Jonah:

"Go to the city of Nineveh," He said. "The people there are not behaving well. Tell them that I will destroy their city if they do not change their bad ways."

"Nineveh!" thought Jonah with a shudder. "I can't go there. It's not a safe place! The people there lie and cheat. Why would they listen to me?"

Jonah decided to run away. "The Lord doesn't need me. He can warn the people of Nineveh all by Himself," he thought.

Jonah hopped on a ship traveling far, far away. He hid below deck and was soon fast asleep.

As soon as the ship set sail, God sent a fierce storm. Lightning flashed! Thunder boomed! Wind tossed the ship from side to side and tall waves crashed!

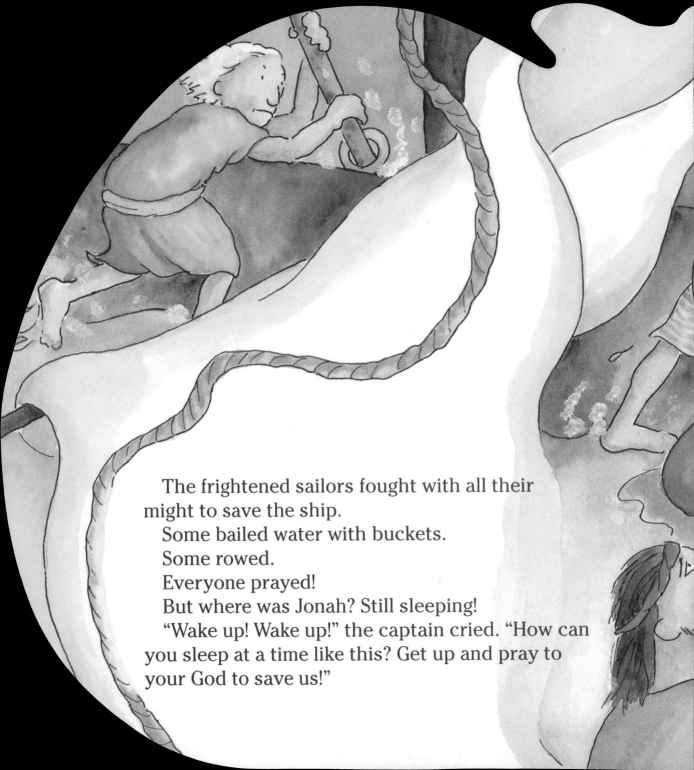

The frightened sailors fought with all their might to save the ship.

Some bailed water with buckets.

Some rowed.

Everyone prayed!

But where was Jonah? Still sleeping!

"Wake up! Wake up!" the captain cried. "How can you sleep at a time like this? Get up and pray to your God to save us!"

Jonah prayed and prayed, but the wind blew harder and the waves grew bigger! Finally he understood—he should have gone to Nineveh!

"God is angry with me," he told the captain. "If you throw me overboard, all your troubles will be over." But the sailors shook their heads. They didn't want to throw anyone into the angry sea!

Just then the highest wave of all came rushing toward them!

"We must save ourselves!" the captain cried. First the sailors prayed for forgiveness for what they were about to do. Then they threw Jonah overboard, into the stormy sea.

In a flash the roaring waters became calm!

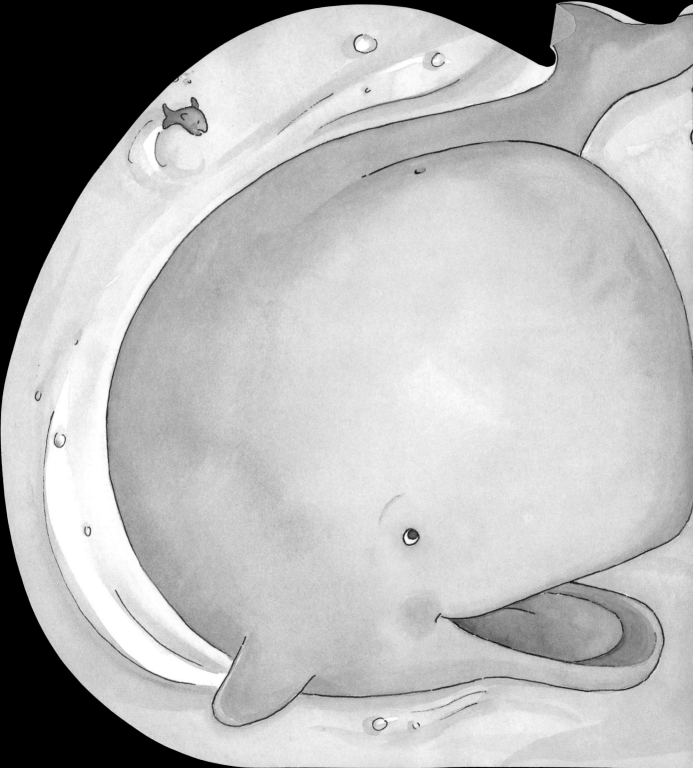

Jonah began to sink below the sea. Just when he thought he would drown, God sent a big whale to the rescue. The big old fellow swallowed Jonah in just one gulp!

Jonah slid down, down, down, until he found himself right in the middle of the beast's huge belly!

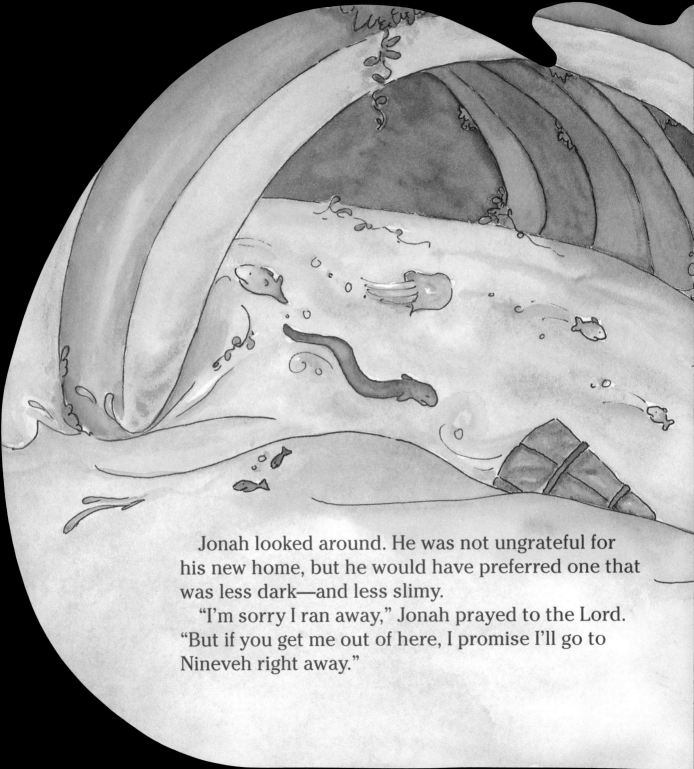

Jonah looked around. He was not ungrateful for his new home, but he would have preferred one that was less dark—and less slimy.

"I'm sorry I ran away," Jonah prayed to the Lord. "But if you get me out of here, I promise I'll go to Nineveh right away."

God decided to give Jonah another chance. So He guided the huge whale toward land and told it to set Jonah free.

A whale-sized cough sent Jonah tumbling out of the enormous beast's belly. He landed on the beach with a *thud*!

Jonah had learned his lesson! He picked himself up and hurried off to Nineveh.

Jonah told the people of Nineveh that God was
very angry with them:

"You have been lying and cheating. You have been
fighting with your neighbors. If you do not change,
God will destroy your city."

The people of Nineveh became quiet and listened to Jonah. Frightened by God's warning, they all rushed home to pray for forgiveness. Jonah couldn't believe it!

After a short while God saw that the people of Nineveh had changed. So He decided to give them another chance, just as He had given one to Jonah.

"The way of the Lord is good," thought Jonah as he started on his long trip home.